Copyright © 2020 Disney Enterprises, Inc. and Pixar. All rights reserved.
Published in the United States by Random House Children's Books,
a division of Penguin Random House LLC, 1745 Broadway, New York, NY 10019,
and in Canada by Penguin Random House Canada Limited, Toronto, in conjunction with
Disney Enterprises, Inc. Random House and the colophon are registered trademarks
of Penguin Random House LLC.

rhcbooks.com

ISBN 978-0-7364-4096-7

Printed in the United States of America

10 9 8 7 6 5 4 3 2 1

Disney·PIXAR

ONWARD

Behold! The Majestic Unicorn

(and Other **Not-So-Magical** Beings)

ILLUSTRATED BY

JEFF PIDGEON & THE DISNEY STORYBOOK ART TEAM

Random House 🏠 New York

LONG AGO, the world was full of WONDER!

Majestic **UNICORNS** and other awe-inspiring beings of all shapes and sizes shared adventure, excitement, and even **MAGIC**.

Over time,
magic faded away.
But even *NOW*, creatures like

the UNICORN inspire

AWE and
WONDER

within any
beholder.

ELVES

were

HEROIC and TRUE,

facing **DANGER**

around

EVERY corner.

And
they are *still*

THE LORDS

of their
domain.

NO
creature
was more
FEROCIOUS
than the
MIGHTY
DRAGON!

Even
today,
TAMING A
DRAGON
is an
IMPOSSIBLE
feat.

Formidable **TROLLS** were **FIERCE PROTECTORS** of their territories.

They *STILL* collect what they're owed.

Majestic **CENTAURS** roamed free across the plains as their manes *blew in the breeze.*

Centaurs continue to bravely traverse
TREACHEROUS terrain.

Graceful **MERFOLK** frolicked in the vast and untamed oceans.

These fair beings still relish the
ADVENTURE of the rocky seas.

Wise

WHISPERING

TREES

took great pleasure in

MOCKING

many
a weary traveler.

The trees *STILL* befuddle
great adventurers who
journey into
their
MYSTICAL
forest home.

Whimsical **SPRITES**

once spread joy and delight
wherever they **FLUTTERED**.

They
remain a

SPIRITED
BUNCH

who fly together
in

HARMONY.

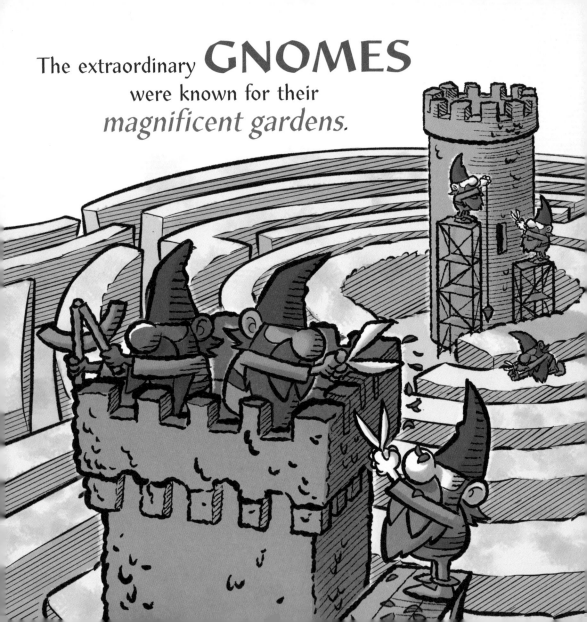

The extraordinary **GNOMES** were known for their *magnificent gardens.*

Their creations *today* evoke AWE
in all who gaze upon them!

While **some things**
have remained the same,
it is true that times have changed.

MAGIC

is more *DIFFICULT* to find.

But if you dig

deep enough...

you can discover it in

UNEXPECTED PLACES.